VIVIAN FRENCH & ALEX AYLIFFE

OH NO, ANNA!

PEACH
ATLANTA

Home from the store.
Time to put things away.

Anna finds a red bucket ...

Oh no,
Anna!

Anna finds some green yarn . . .

Oh no,
Anna!

Anna finds
a yellow cup . . .

Oh no,
Anna!

Anna finds
an orange
orange . . .

Oh no, Anna!

Anna finds
a blue bowl . . .

Oh no,
Anna!

Anna finds
a black pen . . . .

Anna finds a brown tote bag . . .

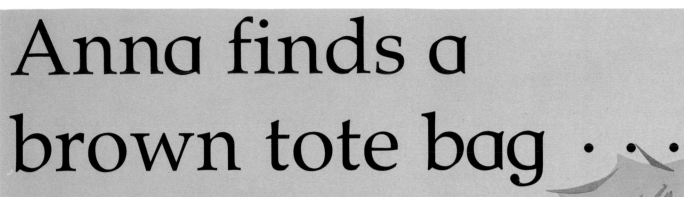

Oh no,
Anna!

Mom
finds . . .

Time to clean up.

Oh yes, Anna!

Anna!